The Birthday Girl

Jean Little

with illustrations by
June Lawrason

ORCA BOOK PUBLISHERS

National Library of Canada Cataloguing in Publication Data

Little, Jean, 1932-
The birthday girl / Jean Little ; with illustrations by June Lawrason.

(Orca echoes)
ISBN 1-55143-292-7

I. Lawrason, June II. Title. III. Series.

PS8523.I77B58 2004   jC813'.54   C2004-900642-8

Library of Congress Control Number: 2004100822

Summary: Nell has a wonderful birthday, so why does the next day have
to be so awful? And where could her cat, Lady Jane Grey, have got to?

Teachers' guide available from Orca Book Publishers.

Orca Book Publishers gratefully acknowledges the support
of its publishing program provided by the following
agencies: the Department of Canadian Heritage, the Canada
Council for the Arts, and the British Columbia Arts Council.

Design by Lynn O'Rourke
Printed and bound in Canada

Orca Book Publishers
PO Box 5626, Stn. B
Victoria, BC Canada
V8R 6S4

Orca Book Publishers
PO Box 468
Custer, WA USA
98240-0468

www.orcabook.com
07 06 05 • 4 3 2

This story is in memory of Nell Mellis, my grandma's first cousin. She really did dress up sunflowers and have a party.

And for Ethel Hindley, my beloved friend, after whom I named Nell's Aunt Ethel.

—J.L.

Chapter One
"Where are you, Lady Jane?"

Nell Mellis finished saying her prayers and hopped into bed. Tomorrow she would be eight. She was so excited that she was sure she would not sleep a wink. She snuggled down and looked for her cat who always slept curled up beside her.

But Lady Jane was nowhere to be seen.

"Good night, honey," her mother said, stooping to kiss her.

"Wait! Where's Lady Jane?" Nell said.

Nell's mother was not fond of cats, but she understood how much her little girl loved her pet. She glanced around the room. The gray and white tabby was not there.

"She'll be along later," Mother said, pulling Nell's

covers up. "You must get to sleep or you'll be too tired to celebrate tomorrow."

"I can't sleep without Lady Jane," Nell declared with a catch in her voice.

"Nonsense," Mother said briskly, as she picked up the lamp and turned to leave. "Remember that the faster you sleep, the sooner your birthday will begin."

"And I will be eight at last," Nell said softly, closing her eyes.

But the moment the door shut, Nell's eyes popped open. How could she sleep with her birthday coming so soon and Lady Jane lost? Mother should know she couldn't.

She lay and thought about the day she had found Lady Jane abandoned in the ditch. Lady Jane was a tiny bedraggled kitten, soaking wet and nothing but bones. She was so young that she fitted easily in Nell's cupped hands. Nell had caught her up and run for the house.

The kitten had been so frail that even Nell's mother saw at once that she could not be left to become a barn cat. They had dripped warm milk into her mouth, but it was hard to get her to swallow.

"We may not be able to save her," Mother had warned. "I can't spend time fussing over her. You'll have to tend her."

"I will save her," five-year-old Nell had declared fiercely. "Wait and see."

She had nursed the scrawny kitten so faithfully that Lady Jane soon grew strong.

"She tags after you like a puppy dog," Aunt Ethel said. "I've never seen the like."

"She knows Nell saved her," Nell's sister said.

Now, remembering Margaret's words, Nell smiled and drifted off to sleep.

Next morning, she thought of her missing cat before she recalled that it was her birthday.

"Lady Jane," she called. "Here, puss."

The sunlight coming through her curtains lit up the covers. But no gray tabby gazed up at her with sleepy golden eyes.

"She must be downstairs," Nell told her two rag dolls. They sat in the old rocker and smiled at her. Those smiles made her remember what day it was. She shot out of bed. She did not take time to put on her robe and slippers. She ran headlong down the stairs to the farm kitchen.

"I'm eight!" she yelled.

Mother turned from the stove to hug her.

"Happy birthday, Nell," she said softly. "May this be your happiest ever."

Chapter Two
Presents

Father and Nell's thirteen-year-old brother Sinclair came in from outside. Father had washed his face at the pump and was drying it. Water drops sparkled in his black curly hair.

Sinclair had not wasted time washing. He raced across the kitchen to give Nell a birthday spank.

"Don't you dare!" Nell shrieked, dodging out of reach.

"Sinclair, go wash. Hurry up," Mother said.

Father bent to give Nell a big kiss. Then he called up the back stairs. "Margaret Anne Mellis, the birthday girl is waiting for her song. See if you can get down here before your brother gets his face washed."

Sinclair ran out to the pump and, in two seconds flat, plunged back into the kitchen, laughing. His hair stood all on end. His hands and face were dripping wet.

"Beat you, sis!" he shouted.

Margaret came downstairs sedately. She was all dressed with her hair combed.

"You didn't dry your hands or wash your ears," she told her brother, "so it doesn't count. You also still smell like the barn."

"Stop it, you two," Mother told them.

Aunt Ethel sat at the parlor organ. She spread her hands across the ivory keys, put her feet on the pedals and began to pump. The organ wheezed into life. When the family gathered, she struck a chord.

"Happy birthday to you," everyone sang.

Nell went pink and ducked her head. But she loved it. Even dressed in nothing but her nightgown, she felt like a queen. She was going to enjoy being eight.

As soon as she found Lady Jane, that is.

"Come on, Nell. Open your presents," Sinclair shouted.

"Not until she's decent," Mother said. "Run up and put on your robe and slippers. Even a birthday girl should not sashay about in front of her father and brother in nothing but her nightdress."

Nell flew back upstairs. She pulled on the robe Aunt Ethel had made for her a year ago. She shoved her feet into the real Indian moccasins Father had brought home from the Hudson's Bay store. Nell loved them. The beading was beautiful and they were lined with rabbit fur and were warm even when the farmhouse was icy cold in winter.

She stopped long enough to glance in the small square of mirror that Father had tacked up over her clothes chest.

"You are eight years old," she told the face in the glass.

She stared at her reflection. Two bright blue eyes, brown tousled braids, a freckled snub nose and a big grin all looked just the same as they had the day before. Being eight should have changed something, but she could not see what. She was still not nearly as pretty as Margaret.

"Oh, well," she said, spinning away from the looking glass and dashing down the stairs once again, going so fast that she almost landed upside-down.

"Easy does it," Father said, catching her and swinging her through the air to her place. "If there's a fire, nobody told me."

Nell was too excited to thank him. It was time to open her presents.

Three parcels waited at her place. She reached for the top one.

"That's from Aunt Ethel and me," Margaret told her.

Nell tore off the pink ribbon and tissue paper. Inside the box lay a new doll with eyes as blue as

Nell's own. She had real hair and a pretty pink dress. She had on a matching coat and bonnet too. The doll in the catalogue had had no coat. Nell guessed at once that Aunt Ethel had made them. And in the box there was a flannel nightgown exactly like Nell's own. The doll's hands and feet were china like her head, but her body was cloth and perfect for cuddling.

Nell gazed at her. She was the doll she had shown Margaret weeks before in the Eaton's catalogue.

"You will have to wait for your birthday," Margaret had said.

"But my birthday isn't until August!" Nell had cried.

Margaret had smiled. "August will come," she had said.

Nell had not believed her, but her sister had been right.

"Aunt Ethel made her the coat and bonnet and nightgown," Margaret said.

Aunt Ethel was Mother's aunt. When Mother's mother had died of typhoid, Aunt Ethel had taken the two-year-old to live with her. She had made all Mother's clothes when Mother was a child. Then, she had come to live with them when Sinclair was a baby and she had sewed for the whole family from then on. Mother hemmed and darned, but Aunt Ethel made the fancy things.

"She's beautiful!" Nell breathed. "I'm going to call her Jocelyn."

Everyone laughed. Jocelyn was the name of Nell's beloved Sunday school teacher. She was young and pretty and she made even the dullest story come to life. She gave prizes too for learning Bible verses. Nell was good at getting things by heart and she had more Bible picture cards than anyone else.

"Miss Douglas will be proud," Margaret said.

"You're forgetting your manners, Nell," Mother reminded gently.

"Thank you both very much," Nell said. Then she

made herself stop opening gifts to go hug Margaret and Aunt Ethel.

Her brother's present was tied with twine. Nell could not undo the knots. Sinclair grinned and cut them with his jackknife. He had bought her a small box of watercolor paints.

Nell gasped in delight. She had never had a box all her own before. The six little squares of color were so bright and beautiful. She could hardly wait to paint a picture. She would do one of her cat.

"Has anyone seen Lady Jane?" she asked, remembering.

"She was in the barn last night," Father said. "What's in that big box, little Nell?"

The large box held a new dress. Nell was not really surprised. Her last good dress was too short, even though Mother had made it with a big hem for letting down.

"You must have grown a foot taller in the past year," Mother had said.

Nell gazed at the dress. It was a plain blue material. The color reminded Nell of the sky in the evening just before it got really dark. The dress was trimmed with lace at the throat and it had pretty pearl buttons up the back. The skirt was gathered so it would twirl.

"We'll put your hair up in rags tomorrow night," Mother smiled.

Nell sighed. The rags were lumpy to sleep on and the bobbing ringlets were always gone by noon. But there was no use fussing. Mother was so fond of those curls. Miss Douglas would also admire them.

"Read the card, missy," Father said. "That's the part I made."

Everyone but Mother laughed as Nell read the message out loud. Mother shook her head, but her eyes twinkled.

For our Birthday Girl
so she will not have to
go to church in her
birthday suit.
Love,
Mother and Father

They were all wonderful gifts. And her birthday was just beginning. Nell danced around the room, holding her new doll high in the air.

"Oh, Jocelyn, it is so glorious to be the birthday girl," she sang. "Perfectly, perfectly perfect!"

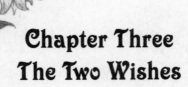

Chapter Three
The Two Wishes

"Now let me comb out your hair before you get your clothes on. When you are dressed I'll have your breakfast waiting," Mother said.

She undid Nell's tousled braids in a flash and plaited two neat ones. Nell felt her forehead pull tight but she was used to it. The braids would start coming loose soon enough. She had soft, slippery hair that made Mother and Aunt Ethel sigh.

"Take your gifts up with you. You needn't wear stockings. Today's going to be another scorcher," Mother said.

In her room, Nell pulled on her drawers and cotton undershirt. Then she wiggled into her everyday dress. She stuck her feet into the old moccasins she wore indoors. They were soft and shapeless, but they protected her toes. They felt so much more comfortable than her Sunday shoes or her school boots.

As she came down, she looked for Lady Jane. She was not curled up by the woodstove. Nell decided to look outside as soon as she was absolutely sure the cat was not somewhere in the house. She searched high and low, in behind old dusty trunks in the small airless attic, under the beds, behind the wardrobes and chests where they kept their clothes. No cat.

Then Mother called her to try on her new dress. She twirled around to make the skirt flare out.

"Do stand still, child," Mother scolded, but she was smiling. She had made the skirt full, knowing how Nell would love making it stand out.

Back in her old clothes, Nell went outside. No cat lurked among the tall cornstalks or slept in the shade behind the rain barrel. She found a frog and two ladybugs but no gray tabby.

"Nell, get in here. You have work to do, birthday or no birthday," Aunt Ethel called.

Nell made a rude face, but really she was glad to get inside where it was slightly cooler. She went to the dipper and got herself a big drink.

"What if Lady Jane ran away?" she asked Aunt Ethel.

"Why on earth would she?" Aunt Ethel said sensibly. "She's so fat she has not even been hunting lately. The mice around here are getting as bold as brass."

Nell grinned and started on her chores. She had to make her bed and dust the parlor furniture. Then she and her mother shelled a big bowl of peas. Nell was pleased with that job, knowing they were for her birthday supper.

Later she carried lunch out to the men in the field. The basket with its thick sandwiches and bottles of cold tea was heavy. Every time she paused to rest, she looked around for Lady Jane, but no cat turned up.

After she dried the noon dishes, she was going out to look again, but Mother told her to stay indoors until it cooled off a little.

Nell painted a picture of Jocelyn.

"I'd know her anywhere," Mother said. "Now go out and pick some flowers for a bouquet before you get your party clothes on."

Nell picked the pansies with the prettiest faces and two white roses to put in the center. Margaret and Sinclair decorated the dining room with pink and blue streamers Mother had bought in Swift Current.

Mother and Aunt Ethel had made Nell a birthday cake the night before. Now they were putting in the favors and icing it with butter icing. They shooed Nell away.

Then it was time to dress. Nell ran and put on her new dress. Mother brushed out her daughter's pigtails and tied her hair back with a new blue ribbon.

When Mother carried in the cake, Nell was so excited she thought she might fly apart. She sat for three whole seconds admiring the eight candles with their tall bright flames. She thought hard about what to wish. Then she knew.

I wish I could find Lady Jane and have another party tomorrow since she did not get to come to this one, she said inside her head. She blew as hard as she could. Every candle winked out. Her wish would come true this year!

"What did you wish?" Father whispered in her ear. "You can tell me."

Nell pushed his head away. "No!" she told him.

There were favors in the cake. Sinclair got the ten-cent piece, which meant he would be rich. Nell got the thimble. Aunt Ethel found Grandmother's ring in hers. Father was left with the button, which meant he would be a bachelor and have to do his own mending.

28

"Mary, don't leave me," he begged.

Even Mother laughed.

"Now for one last surprise," Father said. He had brought home a new songbook. They finished Nell's birthday standing around the organ singing one song for each member of the family. Nell chose "When you come to the end of a perfect day."

She was in bed when she remembered Lady Jane. She had never looked in the barn. What if her cat was there and came out and got caught by a fox? Why hadn't she gone to look?

Almost as soon as she drifted off, she woke in a panic. She had dreamed a pack of huge coyotes was chasing Lady Jane across the prairie. Or were they wolves?

She sat bolt upright and shivered. Why, oh, why hadn't she gone out to look?

You could go right now.

Nell gasped as the shocking words popped into

her head. She COULD NOT go now. It was the middle of the night. The whole house was silent and sleeping. Her cat would be all right until morning.

She lay back down and pulled her covers up over her head. She could not stay under there though. Her heart hammered and her breath came fast. You could go. You could, her brain said again. If you really loved Lady Jane, you would.

Even though it was dark, she knew the way to the barn. A half-moon shone outside her window along with hundreds of stars.

Nell Mellis gulped and sprang out of bed before she grew too frightened. She tiptoed down the stairs. Her heart thudded like a drum. The kitchen, so familiar in daylight, looked strange and spooky in the dark. The wood stove crouched in the corner like a giant beast. It watched and waited. Even the chairs, so friendly all day, had grown far taller since suppertime.

Don't be a scaredy cat, she told herself.

What if they came alive and chased her?

Don't be daft! she snapped at herself and dashed past them, not stopping to look back. She eased open the back door with trembling hands.

The night was filled with a noisy quiet. Nell had never dreamed a silence could be so loud. But the moon and stars shed a comforting glimmer and the barn was not so very far away.

She crept down the porch steps and set her foot on the path. At that very moment the wind rattled through the dry grass, the moon was swallowed by a dark bank of cloud, and a barn owl gave a long, lonely hoot. Nell bit back a shriek and fled to the safety of the porch. She looked back once.

"Lady Jane," she whispered, "stay in the barn. I promise I'll come for you tomorrow."

Something howled. It was far away, but Nell did not stop running until she reached the comforting safety of her very own bed.

"Tomorrow," she choked out. "I will come. I vow."

Chapter Four
Pickles

The next day, Nell pulled on her clothes hit or miss. She must find her cat right this minute. She burst into the kitchen like a firecracker.

"Did anyone see Lady Jane?" she demanded.

"Oh, Nell, don't worry about that cat," Mother said, plunking a bowl of oatmeal down at Nell's place. "Cats always land on their feet. Come and eat."

"Your Lady Jane has only used up a couple of her nine lives," Aunt Ethel said, grinning at her great niece. "No need to fret yet."

Nell remembered Lady Jane's narrow escapes all too clearly. The half-grown kitten had fallen into the rain barrel. Then, later, she had almost been run over by a wagon wheel. She had nearly died.

"She was fine two days ago," she said, scowling at her great aunt. "I'll just run and see if she's in the barn. I can't eat, Mother, until I know she's safe."

Mother caught her shoulder and pushed her down on her chair.

"No, you don't," she said in a firm voice. "Another hour won't matter. After you eat and fetch a pail of water, you can start searching."

"But ..." Nell began.

"But me no buts, young woman. She's a cat, not a lost baby. Eat."

Nell hated it when Mother refused to listen. Usually Nell dawdled over her porridge but not now. She was going to cry if she had to spend one more minute in the same room as her mother. She gulped down a big bite and choked.

Aunt Ethel glanced at her. "Do finish up. We have a lot to do and we need you out from underfoot," she said, trying not to sound cross.

Then Margaret rushed through the kitchen to

peer out the back door. Nell stared at her. Her sister had on her new hat and gloves.

"Where are you going?" she demanded.

Margaret laughed. "I knew you weren't listening yesterday," she said. "I'm going into Swift Current with Arabella. Her sister is taking us in their new buggy."

"Can I come?" Nell asked, forgetting her vow to search for Lady Jane.

"No," Margaret said. "You were not invited and there would not be room in the buggy. We will have to squeeze together as it is."

"Here they come, Margaret," Aunt Ethel said. "Let me straighten that hat. My, you are pretty as a picture."

Margaret blushed. She stood still while their aunt set her hat straight. Her eyes sparkled and her fair hair shone. She bounced out the door, calling, "Good morning!"

Nell scowled. Her sister did not even wave

goodbye. Nobody in her family cared about her now that her birthday was over.

"Who wants to go to stupid old Swift Current?" she muttered.

"Stop begrudging your sister a day off, child," Aunt Ethel scolded. She held out the empty pail. "Now get a wiggle on. We need this filled now, not tomorrow."

Nell pumped for all she was worth. The water spurted into the bucket and flooded over the brim onto the ground. Nell jumped clear. Then she lugged the brimming pail back to the house. She let it down with a bump and water slopped over the edge. Her mother jumped to steady it. She shot Nell a stern look.

"I'm sorry, Nell," she said, her voice sharp, "but you'll have to entertain yourself this morning. Aunt Ethel and I are making pickles."

"I'll help," said Nell, brightening.

"No, dear. You'd just be in the way. Make your bed and then go look for that fool cat."

Mother dropped a hurried kiss on top of Nell's head while she steered her towards the stairs.

"I never have any fun," Nell whined.

"You had a lovely party just yesterday," Aunt Ethel said.

"And making pickles is not fun," Mother snapped. "Once that wood stove heats up, the kitchen becomes an inferno."

"I LIKE BEING HOT!" Nell shouted in her rudest voice. "And I LOVE making pickles."

Mother snorted.

"That is quite enough, miss. Off you go," she said, turning her back on her daughter.

Nell stamped into her bedroom. She yanked up her quilts. She punched her pillow hard. Then, all at once, she realized she was forgetting her vow to Lady Jane, who was not a "fool cat," whatever Mother said.

She raced through the house to the back porch. Then she sat down on the step and changed into her boots. Mother made them wear boots whenever they left the yard since Sinc had pierced his bare foot on a nail and almost died of blood poisoning. Then she was off to the barn.

Lady Jane loved it there. There were mice to chase. There was milk to steal. Nell liked it herself even though she did not care for mice.

"Lady Jane," she called in a coaxing voice, pushing open the big door. "Oh, Lady Jane, where are you?"

"Meww!"

Nell jumped for joy and ran toward the sound.

"Puss, puss," she cried out. "You're safe."

"Meow. "

Something about the second meow made her stop in her tracks and stare all around. Then she saw her brother. He had been hiding in an empty stall. When he jumped out, he was laughing like a loon.

"You are HORRID!" Nell screamed at him. Hot tears burst from her eyes. She whirled around and ran outside, away from him. If Lady Jane had been

there, she would not have stayed, not with Sinc making such a rumpus.

"It was just a joke," Sinclair called after her.

"It is NOT funny," Nell sobbed. "My poor cat has probably been KILLED and all you can do is make jokes."

Sinc ran after her and grabbed her elbow.

"Nellie, I saw her just yesterday," he yelled. "She's not killed. After supper, we will find her for sure." Nell flung her arms around his middle. He smelled of sweat and hay.

"Oh, Sinc, where was she?" she begged, rubbing her wet face on his shirt.

"She was down by the creek," he said, "walking along near that little bluff. She looked very busy. I'm sorry I didn't tell you."

Nell ran back through the barnyard. In her rush, she did not see a puddle left from her journey with the pail. Her foot skidded out from under her and she landed flat on her front in a cow plop.

41

She sprang up and looked down at herself. She was a mess. A disgusting mix of mud and manure was plastered all over the front of her dress.

Sinc stopped to look back at her. She was such a sight that he laughed.

"You BEAST!" Nell screamed. She ran lickety-split to find her mother.

Chapter Five
In Disgrace

Mother was sorry, but she was also highly annoyed. She stripped Nell's dress off right there in the kitchen. Nell began to protest, but her mother paid no attention.

"Nobody's looking, and you are not about to track manure through our clean house," Mother said.

Nell expected to be plopped into the tin tub and scrubbed clean with hot water and soap. Instead she was scrubbed down with a wash rag dipped in cold water in the bucket while she stood on a flour bag. Then, shame-faced and shivering, she was wrapped in an old sheet and sent up to her room to dress.

As she stumbled upstairs, Nell heard Mother say to Aunt Ethel, "What a day for the child to choose!"

"Be fair. The poor chick did not choose," Aunt Ethel said. But Nell could tell she was laughing.

"I'll never forgive them," she told her dolls.

They smiled. They did not order her "out from underfoot."

Nell could not remember feeling so hurt by her family. She was cold too. She should have enjoyed being cool, but she didn't. She pulled on her oldest dress and threw herself down on the bed. Then she sobbed and sobbed. In the end, she cried herself to sleep.

She woke up feeling hot and rumpled and grumpy. What could she do to make herself feel better?

Lady Jane! She had forgotten her again.

She erupted into the kitchen just as Mother was carrying a steaming saucepan of water to where Aunt Ethel waited.

"For pity's sake, Nell! I almost spilled this boiling water over you. Do go outside and don't come back until we're done," she snapped.

"Wait. I've made you a little picnic," Aunt Ethel said, handing Nell a thick sandwich of homemade bread and cheese. "If you're thirsty, get a drink at the pump. We'll call you when we're done."

Nell took the food, but she marched out the door without saying thank you. Aunt Ethel was not giving her a treat. She was getting rid of her. And Mother was just as bad. They were like the cruel stepmother in "Hansel and Gretel."

"I hate them," she whispered, not seeing Aunt Ethel wave to her from the window.

I need Lady Jane in the worst way, she thought. She always understands.

Munching on her sandwich as she went, Nell headed down the edge of the top field to the windbreak. When it was full of fast running water each spring, the creek flowed along beneath a low bank. It had cut into the earth so there was an overhang at the edge. The Mellis children called the highest spot on the overhang the bluff although Father said a real bluff would be much higher. There was no water in the creek now, just some mud left from a quick rain squall the week before.

"Lady Jane," Nell called, looking all around. "Where are you, puss?"

But no cat appeared.

Chapter Six
Danger

Nell inched out to the very edge of the overhang and peered down. As she searched the creek bed for some sign of her cat, a jay screeched in the willow tree nearby. Nell leaped up, and under her feet the earth moved. As she scrambled backwards to safety, Lady Jane came running along the bank. She had something in her mouth. From somewhere beneath the crumbling bank, Nell was horrified to hear crying.

She stood frozen for what seemed like forever. She could not move hand or foot as she watched the earth pull loose and begin to slide into the muddy creek bed below. Everything moved slowly, like things do in nightmares. Then from somewhere beneath the falling mud and grass she heard, once again, the sounds of crying.

Mewing!

"It's kittens!" Nell gasped.

Lady Jane dropped the dead field mouse she was bringing home to eat and sprang down onto the heap of fallen earth. She mewed frantically and pawed at the grass and mud, but she was not strong enough to shift it. In seconds, Nell was beside her, tearing up clumps of earth with both hands and throwing them aside.

"Please, God," she prayed, "help me find them."

Then her scrabbling fingers touched a dirty warm bundle. It was still breathing. She scooped it out and put it next to the mother cat where it went on making small, pitiful noises.

One look at Lady Jane, still frantically digging, told her there were others still buried. She kept clawing at the clumps of grass and mud. Dirt caked in her fingernails. Oh, where were they?

Then she found not one but two more. They were curled together and, when she pulled them free, Lady Jane ran over to her and nosed them thankfully.

One mewed and Nell put it next to the first one she had rescued.

But the third kitten lay limp in her muddy hands.

"Breathe," Nell whispered to it. "Please, breathe."

Instinctively, she squeezed its small ribcage with one hand while she fished out the handkerchief in her pocket. The kitten's nose and mouth were clogged with mud. She brushed the loose dirt off and, spitting on the hanky, washed its small nose clean.

The tiny body shuddered. To Nell's singing joy it came alive in her shaking hands.

"Were there just three?" Nell asked, still anxious.

Lady Jane crouched over the three filthy bundles of fur. She no longer seemed worried. All her kittens were clearly safe. Nell had no doubt her clever cat could count.

All at once, she sank down on the bank next to her busy cat and began to shake. Lady Jane gave her a look. Stop shivering and help! that look said.

Nell spat on her handkerchief again and washed the mud away from the first kitten's tiny face with the closed eyes and flat ears. It was so young it hardly looked like a baby cat, but Nell had seen newborn kittens before.

Finally, Lady Jane began to purr, and a wave of gladness broke over Nell. She and her brave cat had done it. Lady Jane's first litter of kittens was going to survive their brush with death.

Suddenly Lady Jane stopped washing her children. She picked up one kitten by the scruff of its neck and stood looking at Nell.

It took Nell a moment, but she got the message. She lifted the others. Holding them cradled against her front, she followed her cat home.

When she neared the house, Nell slowed down. She could not interrupt the pickle making, even with new kittens. She would wait to surprise them when they finished.

She carried the kittens up onto the back porch and put them in the sagging seat of the wicker rocker. Then she ran out and got the four dusters Mother had hung to dry that morning. They were warm and smelled of sunshine. She found a half-bushel basket that had held apples and padded it with the dusters. Very gently, she lifted the two squirming bundles into the nest she had made. As she did, Lady Jane, still with the first kitten in her mouth, jumped in and curled up around her children. At once, all three butted against their mother, looking for milk. Soon they were sucking away. Lady Jane gave Nell a proud glance before she began washing them thoroughly once more.

"They are lovely, Lady Jane," Nell said. She leaned down to look more closely.

Her cat shifted, her eyes suddenly widening with concern. Nell quickly backed away.

"I won't hurt them," she whispered.

What if her cat grew so nervous she felt she had to move her family again? What if she decided the side porch was not a safe place?

Nell backed around the corner and sat herself down on the top step. Only then did she see that she was covered with dirt. A lot of the overhang had come down on her while she was digging. She stood up and brushed herself off with both hands. Dust flew from her dress. Her boots were white with it. She leaned over and rubbed at them with handfuls of long grass.

Then a new problem presented itself.

Mother did not like cats. How was she, Nell, going to persuade her to keep the kittens? What if she said they must be drowned? Lots of people drowned unwanted kittens.

Then Nell looked up and saw the five sunflowers.

They were tall and splendid lined up by the fence. And they were nodding their heads at her.

"It'll be all right," they seemed to be saying. "You'll think of something."

She had to smile. They looked like a row of tall friendly ladies with brown faces and yellow hair.

She nodded back to them.

"Good afternoon, my dears," she called.

They bowed and twirled a little. Maybe they were curtseying. They liked her! She got up and went over to them. They really did look like fine ladies.

"You only need bonnets," she told them, standing up tall to stroke the bright petals.

Then she remembered seeing another bushel basket, filled with bits and pieces left over from her party, standing just inside the back door. She ran up the steps, eased open the door and slid the basket outside. She stood back and looked at what was in it. Torn streamers and crumpled paper. Long pieces of wrinkled pink ribbon.

Nell Mellis clapped her hands. She took some tissue paper and a thin pink ribbon. With them, she made a hat for the first sunflower. She reached up and fitted it on just so.

"You are Mrs. Beecroft," she said, backing up to see how the lady looked.

Mrs. Beecroft nodded. The other sunflowers watched and waited.

Soon Mrs. Meecroft, Mrs. Shooster, Mrs. Rooster and Miss Frillyface had bonnets too. They all looked wonderful. They looked ready to go to a garden party.

Chapter Seven
Visitors

"All right, all of you," Nell said. "Think hard and get ready while I get Mother."

Nell went to the kitchen window, stood on tiptoe and peered in.

Mother was putting the kettle on. Aunt Ethel was sitting down, mopping her face with her apron. On the table stood a row of jars filled with cucumber pickles. The jelly bag dangled above the biggest stockpot, dripping red juice. The two women looked worn out.

Nell took a deep breath and crossed her fingers.

"Mother," she called through the open window, "there are some ladies out here to see you. I think they've come for tea."

Mother whisked her apron off. She took a quick

look in the mirror above the sink. She patted down her flyaway hair.

"Who on earth?" Nell heard her mutter.

"Somebody with no sense and less manners would be my guess," Aunt Ethel said, biting off the words.

Then Mother crossed the kitchen, opened the screen door and came out on the step. She glanced at Nell and her eyes widened.

"Nell Mellis, not again! How on earth did you get so filthy?" she said.

Nell was furious. She had dusted off the dirt so carefully. Then she remembered her face and her hair. She put up her hand and felt the grit.

"And where are the ladies?" Nell's mother asked.

Nell pointed. Would Mother see the fine ladies? Or would she only see more mess?

"Gracious sakes!" Mother said, her eyes wide.

"They are Mrs. Beecroft, Mrs. Meecroft, Mrs. Shooster, Mrs. Rooster and Miss Frillyface," Nell explained in a shaking voice.

Mother looked from the tall nodding flowers to her daughter's tense face. Nell held her breath.

"Would you like to have a cup of tea with my sister and me?" Nell's mother asked the flowers at last in her company voice.

Nell had been so excited about the kittens and then the party flowers. Now she felt messy and not fit for this pretend tea party. She brushed at her hair with both hands. For one moment, all her hurt feeling surged back. Tears sprang into her eyes.

Then her mother reached out and pulled her little girl close, dirt and all.

"I'm sorry, baby," she said. "You've had a hard day."

The back door opened again. Aunt Ethel was coming out, carrying three cups and some leftover birthday cake on a tray.

"Let's all have tea out here," she said. "It's hot here, but not half as hot as that kitchen."

Mother sank down in the rocker where the kittens had been just minutes before.

"Aunt Ethel, you are inspired," she said. "And Nell has more guests—but they don't need cups. Right, Nell?"

Nell turned to look at the flower ladies. Mrs. Beecroft and her friends were all nodding their heads.

"They only drink dew," she said.

Aunt Ethel waved to the sunflowers when she was introduced. She poured the tea and passed the cake around. Finally, she sat back and smiled at her niece. "Not everyone is lucky enough to have two birthday parties," she said.

Nell's eyes lit up.

"I know," she said. "And I have more guests. Put down your tea for a minute and come see."

The two women groaned. They were both very tired and hot.

"Nell, we are tuckered out," her mother said.

"Please. You've got to!" Nell pleaded.

Aunt Ethel set down her cup on the wide railing.

"Come on, Mary," she said. "Nell's had a hard day too."

Nell led her mother and great-aunt around to the side porch. She crossed her fingers for luck and pointed at the basket.

Lady Jane Grey looked up at them, very pleased with herself. Curled around her were three tiny, squeaky-clean kittens.

"Oh my!" Mother said, staring at the tiny creatures.

Nell thought of the sunflowers and knew what to try. She talked fast. "I named the black one Pickles," she said. "When he's big enough, he'd like to live in the barn. And the all gray one can go to Arabella. I heard Margaret say she wants a cat."

"How about the other one? She's going to look just like her mother," Aunt Ethel said.

"Her name's Mary," Nell said in a rush. "Lady Jane wants to name her after Mother—and I want to keep her."

Nobody spoke for a long moment. Then Aunt Ethel laughed out loud and Mother groaned again.

"Is Mary a good mouser?" she asked.

Nell flung her arms around her mother's waist.

"The best," said the birthday girl.